This book belongs to

....

the World's Greatest
Grandma!

Put a photo
of your own
Grandma
here.

→

Written by Kath Smith
Illustrated by Steve Lavis
Designed by Chris Fraser at Page to Page

This is a Parragon Book
First published in 2005

Parragon
Queen Street House
4 Queen Street
Bath BA1 1HE, UK

Copyright © Parragon 2005

ISBN 1-40544-420-7

Printed in China

World's Greatest Grandma

Written by Kath Smith ❀ Illustrated by Steve Lavis

I love going to Grandma's house.
We always have such fun together!

She's really good at playing games...
especially hide and seek!

Usually I hide, and Grandma looks for me.

She always finds me in the end!

Grandma lets me do things that my Mum won't.
She even lets me take photos with her camera.

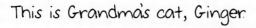
Taking photos is tricky.
Grandma kept moving
when I clicked the
button!

This is Grandma's cat, Ginger.

Here's one that I took of Grandma.

Mum says Grandma spoils me.

Grandma knows how to make proper milkshakes too!

Grandma makes yummy cakes!
She makes extra big ones for me,
and a special small one for Billy Bear.

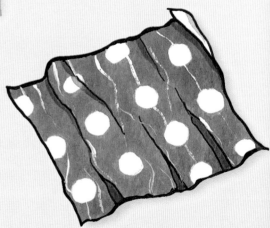

But I think we just like to eat the same things!

We love looking at photos together. Our favourite ones are of Mum when she was very little.

They make us giggle!

This is Billy Bear with my mum
when he was younger.
Grandma lets me play with him
when I go to her house.

I love hearing Grandma's stories about the olden days – especially the one about her wedding day.

Grandma says it was very windy the day she got married.

Grandma's still got the wedding dress she wore.

I wasn't even born then!

These are pressed flowers from Grandma's wedding bouquet - they're practically antique!

I think Grandma looked ever so beautiful!

I'm never bored when I'm with Grandma.
Even when we have to go shopping,
she makes it...

Grandma gave me a shopping
list – in code! Can you guess
what I had to find?

...FUN!

Grandma knows exactly what I like to eat.

She makes great picnics!

Grandma's picnic basket is amazing! It's got EVERYTHING in it!

Guess which sandwich is mine!

Even the animals like Grandma's picnics...

...and we don't mind sharing.

Ginger's been looking in the album again!

Grandma always makes plenty to go round.

Grandma never forgets Billy Bear!

Grandma always has time to play with me.

Grandma and I made this sandcastle together!

She says it's the best sandcastle we have ever built!

Even when she's too tired to play, she still joins in.

And if I'm feeling sad, Grandma knows...

Grandma bought me an ice lolly...

  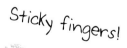

Sticky fingers!

...but I dropped it!

...just how to cheer me up!

Sometimes, I have to help Grandma, now she's getting older.

I can carry my own stuff now.
Grandma says I am a big help.

I help sort out the things we collect.

But I don't mind...

...because she's the
World's Greatest Grandma!